DISNEY'S
KIM POSSIBLE

Adapted by Jasmine Jones
Based on the series created by
Mark McCorkle & Bob Schooley

Watch it on
DISNEY CHANNEL
abc Kids

DISNEY PRESS

VOLO

New York

Printed in the United States of America

First Edition
3 5 7 9 10 8 6 4 2

Library of Congress Catalog Card Number: 2002095480

ISBN 0-7868-4588-0
For more Disney Press fun, visit www.disneybooks.com
Visit DisneyChannel.com

CHAPTER 1

Humiliation Nation

Ski trip!

The biggest field trip of the year was about to begin, and Kim Possible was psyched. She looked around the school parking lot. Everyone was wearing parkas and ski caps. Like her, they were totally ready to jump onto the yellow bus and head for the snow-covered slopes.

I'll really miss the drab hallways of Middleton High School, thought Kim. *Not!*

"Let's keep it moving, people!" Mr. Barkin, their teacher, bellowed. He was holding a clipboard and checking off names as students boarded the bus.

Kim's best friend, Ron Stoppable, joined the crowd of students. He was carrying two long skis over his shoulder.

"Stoppable!" Mr. Barkin said as he stepped in front of Ron. "Stow that gear!"

"Aye, aye, Mr. Barkin!" Ron said. He gave

Mr. Barkin a cheerful salute. Then he spun toward the side of the bus and just missed whacking a kid in the head with his skis.

"Hey!" the kid shouted.

Ron spun again—to tell the kid, "My bad!" This time his skis nearly whacked *Kim* in the head!

"Ron!" Kim shouted.

Ron looked back sheepishly. "Sorry, K.P.," he said, finally tilting his skis upright and out of head-whacking range. "I am just totally psyched."

"Tell me about it," Kim said. "It's been so long since I've skied without some crazed henchman after me."

For Kim, skiing away from henchmen was only one small part of saving the world on a regular basis. As a teenage global crime fighter, Kim often found herself dealing with crazed villains, evil plots, and lots of exploding things, too.

 Suddenly, a nearly naked rodent popped out of Ron's pocket. It was Ron's beloved pet, Rufus. He was wearing a teeny little scarf and matching hat. "Whoo-hoo!" Rufus cried, punching his tiny front paws in the air.

Kim was no fan of hairless rodents. But for a mole rat, Rufus was pretty cool.

"Naked mole rat good to go," Ron said, patting Rufus's head.

Just then, Ron and Kim caught sight of one of the kids waiting to board the bus. He was the only kid who looked ferociously miserable.

"Oh, look, Ron," Kim whispered.

"Alan Platt," Ron said with a knowing nod. "He deserves our pity, K.P."

"So sad," Kim agreed.

"The biggest trip of the school year . . ."

". . . and his parents are the chaperones," Kim finished.

Ron looked grimly at the ground. "Humiliation nation."

"Tragic," Kim said. She closed her eyes and observed a brief moment of silence. "But better him than me!" she finished brightly.

"Kimmie!" a voice shouted.

"Mom?" Kim's mouth dropped open at the sight of her mother's outfit. She was wearing an old red parka that was so puffy, she

looked like a parade float. And the matching hat actually had a pom-pom on it. For sure, a winter fashion *don't.*

"What's the sitch, Mom?" Kim asked, trying not to cringe. Her mother may have been a brilliant brain surgeon, but her fashion sense was limited to lab coats and hospital scrubs. "Did I leave something at home?"

"Not at all, honey," said Dr. Possible. "Your friend Bonnie called us." Dr. Possible glanced at Bonnie, who had just come trotting over.

Bonnie was on Kim's cheerleading squad, and she was waving a little too cheerily at the moment. Kim narrowed her eyes suspiciously.

Calling Bonnie a "friend" was stretching it.

The girl loved to cause trouble, especially for Kim. So a *happy* Bonnie was a *dangerous* thing.

"The Platts came down with the flu at the last minute," Dr. Possible continued.

Hearing this, Alan Platt grinned and high-fived the girl in line behind him. He was back in Normal Land.

Kim's dad walked over. He was a doctor, too—of rocket science. To Kim's dad, "being cool" meant adjusting the room's temperature in Celsius. He was wearing a red parka just as old and ridiculously puffy as Kim's mom's—in other words, it was the "his" version of the winter fashion *don't*.

"So we grabbed our gear, dropped the boys at Nana's, and hightailed it right over," he told Kim.

Kim's eyes grew round as the reality of this nightmare dawned on her. "Wait," she said, hoping that there might be some mistake. "You don't mean . . ."

"Meet our new ski-trip chaperones!" Bonnie announced as she whipped out a digital camera. "Smiles!"

Kim's dad pulled Kim between himself and his wife as Bonnie snapped the picture. Everyone was grinning—but Kim.

A few minutes later, Kim's parents left to grab the rest of their gear, and Ron went to store his skis, leaving Kim alone with Bonnie.

"Wow," Bonnie said. "You know, it just occurred to me that some people might find it humiliating to have their parents along on a class outing." She dangled her camera in front of Kim's face and smiled evilly. "Especially someone with a big photo spread in the yearbook."

"You did this to me on purpose, Bonnie," Kim snapped.

"You are so paranoid," Bonnie huffed, rolling her eyes. "I think your parents are" —she glanced over to where Kim's father stood holding a strange case—"cute."

Kim frowned. This was *so* not the good time.

"Whatcha got there, Dr. P?" Ron asked, pointing to the case.

"My homemade snowboard," Dr. Possible explained. As an expert in astrophysics, he was always inventing things. "I'm ready for shreddy!" Dr. Possible said, grinning at Ron.

Ron looked horrified at this parental use of teen lingo. "Excuse me?" Ron said.

"Dad's trying to act cool," Kim groaned and rolled her eyes in total embarrassment. "I'm doomed."

CHAPTER 2

Beastly Bus Ride

"Ooh!" Kim's mom said brightly, clapping her gloved hands. "I know a fun travel game that Kimmie used to love on family trips!"

"When she wasn't begging for a rest stop, that is," Kim's father added.

Everyone on the bus cracked up. Everyone but one person.

Kim sat toward the rear of the bus, glowering. The scenery was gorgeous—snow-covered trees and sky-high mountains—but

Kim didn't care. She was too busy thinking of ways to disappear from this trip without anyone noticing.

Ron sat next to her, reading the newspaper. "Incredible!" he said.

"I know," Kim agreed through clenched teeth. "Bonnie *will* pay for this."

"No, I mean *this*," Ron said, shoving the *Weekly Wonder* newspaper at her. "Check it out, K.P. We're heading straight into the lair of the Beast."

"'The Snow Beast of Mount Middleton Makes Tracks,'" Kim read aloud. She peered at the blurry photo below the headline. Rufus

looked at it, too, whimpering in fear. Kim had to admit, it *could* have been a picture of the tracks of some strange animal. It also could have been an aerial photo of North Dakota. Or a close-up of someone's problem skin. Or anything else in the world!

"Right," Kim told Ron. "From the same hard-hitting journalists who broke the Frog Boy story."

"I was personally touched by Frog Boy's struggle to fit into a world that could never truly accept him," Ron said seriously.

"Ron—" Kim said as she shoved the paper back at him. "*Look* at this picture. It could be *anything*."

"That's why the *Wonder* is offering five thousand dollars for a clear photo of the Beast!" Ron cried.

Just then, Ron looked around. Everyone on the bus was staring at him.

"You don't really believe all that hooey, do you, Stoppable?" Mr. Barkin asked from his seat behind Ron.

"Thank you, Mr. Barkin," Kim said. She frowned at Ron. "Some of us have *real* issues to deal with this weekend."

Ron lifted his eyebrows. "Like helping your parents with a sing-along?" he asked, pointing toward the front of the bus.

"Here we go!" chirped Kim's mom.

"Join in, Kimmie!" called her dad. He turned to the kids near him and dropped his voice to a whisper. "Did you know that Kim has a beautiful singing voice?" He put his arm around his wife, and they began to sing. "Ninety-nine bottles of pop on the wall, ninety-nine bottles of pop . . ."

Ron happily joined in. "You take one down, pass it around . . . ninety-eight bottles of pop on the wall. Ninety-eight bottles of pop . . ."

Soon everyone was singing. And Kim slid slowly down in her seat.

This was going to be the longest weekend of her life.

CHAPTER 3

Things Go Downhill

"Make sure you collect all your personal belongings!" Kim's dad called to the students on the bus. They had just pulled up to the ski lodge.

After leaving the bus, Ron strapped a huge pack onto his back.

"Ready to find that Snow Beast?" a low voice asked him. He turned to see Mr. Barkin towering over him.

"Mr. B?" said Ron. "I thought you—"

Mr. Barkin clapped a meaty palm over Ron's mouth. "Stoppable, do you want the whole class going after the five Gs?"

"Oh . . . I gotcha," Ron said after Mr. Barkin removed his hand. Rufus got it, too. The mole rat rubbed his fingers together in the universal "show me the money" sign.

"What about Rufus?" Ron asked. Certainly his pet deserved a share.

"Tell you what, Stoppable—" Mr. Barkin said. "You help me get that photo, and I'll cut you in for two percent." He held up two fingers. "How you divvy it with your hairless pal is your business."

"Deal!" Ron said, with a crafty smile, as though he'd just struck an incredible bargain. "Catch you later, K.P.!" he called to Kim.

"Ron? Where are you going?" There was desperation in Kim's voice. He *couldn't* leave her alone in humiliation nation!

"That reminds me of the cutest Kimmie story!" Kim's mom said—*loudly*.

". . . So, we're on our first family ski trip," Dr. Possible was saying to Bonnie and a group of kids. "Kimmie's two years old and she takes off her clothes in the middle of the lodge. . . ."

Kim hadn't felt this much panic since the evil Dr. Drakken threatened to melt her with magma!

Time to take control of this situation, Kim decided. Quickly, she pulled her mother aside. "Mom! Not now. Not ever," she cried.

"Oh, honey," said Dr. Possible. "Two-year-olds have been known to strut around stark naked." She laughed and looked over Kim's shoulder. "Am I right?"

"Absolutely," Bonnie agreed, smiling smugly at Kim. "Please, go on!"

CHAPTER 4

Barkin Breaks the Ice

"**S**houldn't we have mules or Sherpas or something?" Ron asked as he trudged through the snow after Mr. Barkin. They had only been walking for twenty-three minutes, but to Ron, it seemed like weeks.

Rufus giggled from his place on the top of Ron's backpack. To Rufus, Ron *was* the Sherpa!

"When I snow-hike with Kim, we get Sherpas," Ron went on. Of course, Ron's snow adventures with Kim were usually in exotic places like Nepal. And she was the one who did most of the planning.

"You're not traveling with the pep squad today, son," Mr. Barkin snapped as he climbed to the top of a small hill. "Up here, you gotta earn your two percent. . . . Wait a minute. . . ." Mr. Barkin stopped in his tracks. "You hear something?"

Ron glared at the teacher. "Teeth chattering? Knees knocking? Bladder sloshing? That's *me!*"

Barkin held his finger to his lips. "Shh . . . Listen."

Just then, the pine trees shook, and a roar thundered across the mountain.

"Snow Beast!" Ron and Mr. Barkin shouted. Their prize photo—not to mention fame and fortune—was straight ahead!

Mr. Barkin started running. "Get a move on, Stoppable!" he called.

"It's on! It's on!" Ron cried, sprinting.

Mr. Barkin pointed. "Over there."

"Wait!" Ron noticed some trees moving, off to their right. "It changed direction!"

He and Mr. Barkin lunged toward the moving trees. Just then, the ground beneath their feet gave way, and they slid down a steep slope. Suddenly, the slope came to an end. "Whoa!" they screamed as they shot over the edge of a sheer cliff. Far below, a deep bank of snow broke their fall.

Ron sat up, shaking the snow out of his face. Amazingly, he wasn't hurt—his landing had been pretty soft. "Rufus!" Ron cried, noticing a small mole rat-shaped hole in the snow beside him. "Rufus, you okay?"

Rufus sat up. "Mmm-hmm."

"Where's Mr. Barkin?" Ron asked.

The snow beneath Ron started to move. Then it picked him up and shoved him out of the way! Ron suddenly realized *why* he'd had such a *soft* landing—he'd fallen on top of Mr. Barkin!

Mr. Barkin grunted and shook himself. "It got away!" he cried.

Suddenly, there was another thunderous roar. Rufus whimpered and darted behind Ron.

"I-I-It's coming back!" Ron stammered as a creature stepped in front of them. Ron let out a terrified yell.

"Calm down, Stoppable!" Mr. Barkin said. "It's a woman."

The woman gave a little wave. "Thanks for noticing." She was a rather wide woman with glasses and a gap between her two front teeth. She had a hideous bowl haircut and was dressed in drab shades of brown. A strange stuffed animal dangled from a piece of string around her neck. It looked like a tiny otter with wings.

"Well . . . you know . . ." Mr. Barkin said. "You're obviously . . . you know, female."

"We thought you were the Snow Beast," Ron told the woman.

"Not that you look beastly in any way, ma'am," Mr. Barkin added quickly.

"Oh, puh-leeze!" the woman scoffed. "Don't tell me you believe that silly tale."

"No-no-no," Mr. Barkin said, hiding the camera behind him.

"Oh, no," Ron agreed.

"I'm Amy Hall," the woman said. "Pleased to meet you, Mr . . . ?"

"Barkin. Steve Barkin."

Amy stepped closer to Mr. Barkin and batted her eyelashes at him. "Say, Steeeevie—"

"I prefer Steve," Mr. Barkin said.

"That makes two of us," Amy said coyly. "Rrrrrowr. Anyhoo, I got all turned around up here. Would you mind leading me back to the lodge?"

"Actually, we—" Mr. Barkin began.

"Would be tickled pink!" Ron finished.

Amy giggled and punched Mr. Barkin in the arm. "Pink is my favorite color!"

Mr. Barkin rubbed his arm. "Excuse us," he growled. He pulled Ron away. "What about the photos?"

"The photos can wait, Mr. B. You got a lady on the line," Ron said, gesturing toward Amy.

"Stoppable—" Mr. Barkin began.

"Stevie," Amy called, "the lodge awaits us."

"Mr. Barkin: babe magnet," Ron teased.

"Drop it, Stoppable," Mr. Barkin warned. Then he stomped over to Amy. "Ma'am," he said, "please follow me."

"To the ends of the earth, Stevie," Amy promised as she toddled after him.

They walked quickly, none of them hearing the horrible roar that came from the trees behind them.

CHAPTER 5

Code Red

"So, you built your own snowboard, Dr. Possible?" Bonnie asked as she peered at Dr. Possible's strange case.

Kim's father grinned. "You'd be surprised at what you can cobble together with odds and ends from around the Space Center."

"I'd love to see it in action," Bonnie said. She whipped out her digital camera. A picture of Dr. Possible's monstrosity would be a

great addition to her "humiliate Kim" yearbook spread.

Seeing the camera, Kim snowboarded
over. "Whoa! Slow down there, Dad!" Kim
said.

"Kimmie?" said Dr. Possible.

Kim hopped off her snowboard and pulled
her father aside. This was a code red situation. She had to handle it just right, or it
could end in major embarrassment.

"Yours is so much cooler than everyone
else's," Kim said carefully. "You don't want
to bum out the other guys, do you?"

"Gosh," said Dr. Possible, "I don't want to
bum anybody out. Not me."

"Good, Dad. Real good," said Kim.

Okay, she thought, situation normalized. Kim smiled at her dad, then stomped off to talk to Bonnie.

"Is everything okay, Kim?" Bonnie asked, her voice full of fake concern. "You seem kind of stressed."

Kim gritted her teeth. Suddenly, there was a shout from halfway up the slope.

"Kim!" Ron cried as he snowboarded toward them. His arms were waving wildly, like he was out of control. At the last moment, he cut into the snow sharply to stop.

"Ahhh!" Bonnie shouted as a wave of snow whooshed over her. "You did that on purpose!" she told Ron.

Kim smiled. She knew Ron was an excellent snowboarder. Bonnie was right—he'd sprayed that snow on purpose. But Kim wasn't about to let Bonnie know that. "Now who's paranoid, Bonnie?" Kim said. "It was an accident."

Bonnie growled and stormed off.

Once she was gone, Ron stopped flailing. He stood up straight, grinning.

"I owe you one," Kim told him.

"Aww . . . it was nothing," said Ron.

"Find your snow monster?" Kim asked.

Rufus poked his head out of Ron's pocket and shook his head. "Uh-uh."

Ron shushed his naked mole rat and leaned toward Kim. "How much do you know?"

Kim shook her head.

Just then, Mr. Barkin wandered by with the new president of his fan club—Amy.

"I'm gonna buy Y-O-U a mug of hot cocoa, Stevie," Amy said.

"That's really not necessary," Mr. Barkin said. "I need to get back to the slopes."

"With mini-marshmallows," Amy sang.

Just then, Kim noticed the weird stuffed animal hanging on a string around Amy's neck. "Hey," Kim said as Amy walked past, "an OtterFly."

"That's right!" Amy said eagerly. She took off her necklace and showed it to Kim. "You collect Cuddle Buddies?"

Kim was suddenly aware of three things. Number one: some kids from her class—including Bonnie—were building a snowman behind her. Number two: they were *hearing* this conversation. And number three: Cuddle Buddies were ferociously nerd-tacular. "Well," Kim hedged as she glanced over her shoulder, "I've seen them at the mall. No big."

"'*Seen* them'?" Kim's mom repeated as she walked over. She smiled and petted Amy's OtterFly. "Kimmie went *wild* for those little things."

Kim winced. She glanced at her classmates. Yep, they were listening. This was *so* not helping her coolness rating.

"I'm the past president of the Cuddle Buddy Collector's Club!" Amy cried, shaking Kim's hand and pulling her into a hug. "It's so nice to find a fellow Cuddler."

Suddenly, there was a flash of light. Kim looked over her shoulder in horror. Bonnie stood there with her digital camera. "You two must have *so* much in common," Bonnie said snidely.

Kim managed to escape from Amy's bearlike hug, but stopping Amy's mouth was another story. "You meet the nicest people at Cuddle functions, don't you?"

Kim shook her head. "I've never—"

"So, Kimmie, who's your fave?" Amy went on. "Mine's OtterFly, *obviously*!"

Kim blushed and tapped her head as

though she were thinking. How could she stop the humiliation? She didn't want everyone at school to think she was a huge Cuddle Buddy nerd. "Well, it was a long time ago—"

"What was that one you would never let me wash?" Kim's mom asked.

Kim froze. "I don't—"

"Pandaroo!" Dr. Possible said. "That's it. You still sleep with that little guy, don't you? So cute. Lil' Pandaroo."

Behind her, Kim heard Bonnie giggle evilly. Kim could imagine the photo in the yearbook already, with the caption: *Kim Possible, who still sleeps with her fave Cuddle Buddy,*

Pandaroo.

Would the embarrassment never end?

Beasties Bust Out

Ron found Kim at the lodge café, leaning over the outdoor railing. "Kim?" he asked gently.

"Bonnie knows about Pandaroo," Kim said, gazing at the sky. "Hope is lost."

"That's harsh. . . ." Ron said. "Can I borrow the Kimmunicator?"

"Your concern touches me," she said as she handed the communicator to Ron.

Ron pressed a button and spoke into it. "Wade? What's the Snow Beast sitch?"

Wade appeared on the screen. He was the ten-year-old genius who helped Kim and Ron on their adventures. "I've got no historical sightings," said Wade. "No local legends . . . nothing."

"You pulled Wade in on this?" Kim asked.

Ron leaned toward Kim. "Only if he delivers," he whispered.

"What were you talking about?" Wade asked, once Ron took his thumb off the Kimmunicator screen.

"Not about the *Weekly Wonder* reward, if that's what you're thinking," Ron said.

"Barkin already has me down for ten percent," Wade said.

"TEN?" Ron cried. He was only getting two—and he had to split it with Rufus!

"*If* I deliver," Wade added.

"Fine," Ron snapped. "Call me if you find anything." He clicked off the Kimmunicator and held it out toward Kim.

"Keep it," Kim said with a sigh. "Wade might want to share some Beastie breakthrough."

"You want to come with me and Barkin to track it?" Ron asked.

"Don't you get it, Ron?" Kim cried. "This weekend is now strictly damage control. If I don't stay on top of my parents every minute, I'll never be able to show my face in school again! I'm in humiliation nation!"

Kim was so upset she didn't even notice her father. He had walked into the café and had heard every word.

"Let's move, Stoppable," Mr. Barkin said as he walked up to them. "Before that Amy woman force-feeds me cocoa again."

Ron, Mr. Barkin, and Rufus trudged back up the ski slopes.

"I think we're getting close," Ron said when he spied a giant footprint in the snow.

Mr. Barkin grinned and snapped photos of the footprints. Just then, the trees rustled. "Something moved," Mr. Barkin said.

"It didn't sound Beast-sized," Ron said.

Suddenly, something scrambled out from behind some low tree branches.

"Just a dog. Hey, pup," Mr. Barkin said. The animal hopped through the snow, which was almost up to its neck. "What are you doing way out here?"

Mr. Barkin moved to pet the little pup on the head, and the dog reached out its paw— only there was no paw. The dog's paws had been replaced with red, lobsterlike claws!

"CHEESE 'N' CRACKERS!" Mr. Barkin shouted as the claws snapped at him.

"Now *that's* a mixed breed," Ron cried, staring at the half-dog half-lobster.

The dog snapped its claws again, then scurried across the snow on its six short lobster legs. Remembering the *Weekly Wonder* paycheck, Mr. Barkin raised his camera. He ran after the strange creature, snapping photos.

Suddenly, there was a deafening roar. Something big burst through the trees. It looked like a cross between a bear, a rabbit, and a rhinoceros. And it was snarling and roaring at them!

Ron froze, paralyzed with fear. "Snow Beast," he said in a tiny voice, dropping the Kimmunicator.

"No!" cried a voice behind them. Suddenly, the creature calmed down.

"You naughty, naughty beastie!" Amy cooed as she walked over to the creature. She was holding the lobster-dog in her arms, and two figures in ski masks and goggles stood behind her. "You shouldn't have run off like that," Amy scolded the beast. "You had Mommy all worried!"

The Snow Beast fell backward on his haunches and wailed.

"Amy!" Ron said, grinning. "In the nick of time! You tamed the Beast! You saved me!" He gave her a huge hug.

"Why did it listen to her?" Mr. Barkin asked suspiciously as he walked over. "And why did she say, 'Mommy'?" Mr. Barkin added.

Hmmm, thought Ron. Mr. Barkin had a point.

"Oooh, you're a clever one, Stevie," Amy said. Then she turned to one of the masked figures. "Get the camera!" she commanded.

As Mr. Barkin struggled with the masked figure, he yanked off the man's ski mask. Only it wasn't a man. He had the *body* of a man, but the head of a chicken!

Behind him, the other masked figure pulled off his ski mask, revealing a pig head.

Mr. Barkin was still gaping at the chicken-man when the pig-man hit him over the head with a rock. Then pig-man slung Mr. Barkin over his shoulder.

"Take them to the lab," Amy sang as chicken-man picked up Ron.

"Let me go!" Ron shouted, dangling in the air. The chicken-man was pretty strong, considering he was just oversized poultry.

They all followed Amy, who climbed onto the back of the Snow Beast and disappeared over the white landscape.

None of them noticed the tiny telescope that popped up from the snow behind them. It was the Kimmunicator. Wade was peering through the electronic eye.

"Ron?" Wade asked as he caught sight of the strange figures carrying Ron and Mr. Barkin across the snow. "Mr. Barkin?"

Wade began typing frantically on his keyboard. "I'll get Kim!"

Suddenly, two tiny skis popped out of the bottom of the Kimmunicator. Wade hit the EMERGENCY JET-SKI button, and the Kimmunicator sailed toward the lodge.

CHAPTER 7

Things Get Splice-y

Back at the lodge, Kim's father was putting the final touches on a snowman. He stuck a carrot right in the center of the snowman's face just as two of Kim's classmates walked over.

"Nice outfit, Dr. Possible," one of the girls said, eyeing his ridiculously puffy parka. "It's, like, retro chic."

"Groovy," Dr. Possible said sincerely.

49

The girls cracked up at the old-folks slang and walked off.

Suddenly, Kim's father heard a noise behind him. He turned and saw Kim with her hand over her eyes, shaking her head.

"I was making small talk," Dr. Possible said defensively. "Forgive me if that's out-of-bounds."

Kim looked at him. She was surprised at his angry tone. "What do you mean?"

"We better be going, dear," Kim's mom said as she walked up behind her husband. She put her hand on his arm and frowned at Kim. "We wouldn't want Kimmie to be in 'humiliation nation.'"

Kim's eyes widened. "You *heard* me?"

Her parents just turned and walked away.

Kim sighed and looked at the sky. "Smooth move, Kim," she told herself.

Suddenly, something skied into her foot.

"Kim!" Wade's voice cried from the Kimmunicator.

"Wade?" Kim said in disbelief.

"We've got a situation," Wade said.

What a relief, thought Kim. Whatever the sitch, it *had* to be better than her current one!

"You can't just go gallivanting all over the mountain!" Amy scolded the Snow Beast once they were back at her laboratory. "Imagine what people must think."

Mr. Barkin, Ron, and Rufus were strapped against metal tables on the opposite side of the lab.

"What is this place?" Mr. Barkin asked as he looked around the enormous space. There were machines everywhere.

"Just my homey little genetics engineering lab," Amy explained brightly. "Let me show you my favorite part." She leaped over to a wall and twirled around. She hit a switch, and a bank of lights blinded Ron and Mr. Barkin.

"Sweet mother-of-pearl . . ." Barkin said, blinking. When his eyes adjusted to the bright lights, he saw Amy again. She was standing in front of row upon row of stuffed animals.

"Every Cuddle Buddy ever made," Amy said proudly, gesturing toward the collection behind her.

"That's a lot of plush, lady," Mr. Barkin said.

"I collected them all," Amy continued. Suddenly, her tone changed, and she balled her hands into fists. "But it wasn't enough—"

A timer dinged.

"Cookies!" Amy singsonged happily as she walked toward the oven.

"Uh, question," Ron said, still strapped to his table.

"Yes?" Amy asked, pulling on a pair of oven mitts.

"What's up with the monsters?" Ron nodded toward the pig-man, the chicken-man, the lobster-dog, and the bear-rabbit-rhino-Snow-Beast thing.

"I wanted more," Amy said as she pulled a tray of cookies out of the oven. "To go where no Cuddler has gone before." She grinned crazily. "Life-sized living Cuddle Buddies!"

"That's quite a leap," Mr. Barkin said from his table.

"Not if you're one of the world's foremost biogeneticists," Amy chirped. "They called me DNAmy." She walked over and held out her tray of cookies. "They said I was mad at Cuddle Con! Gingersnap?"

Mr. Barkin narrowed his eyes. "Lady, you are . . ."

"Special?" Amy guessed.

"SICK!" Mr. Barkin yelled. "And WRONG!"

Amy was so startled, she dropped her cookies.

"You're just a meanie, Stevie," Amy said with a pout. Then an evil smile slowly spread across her face. "But I can fix that."

CHAPTER 8

Mr. Barkin Gets Ugly

Kim snowboarded across the slopes. When she reached the highest peak, she pulled out the Kimmunicator.

"Wade," Kim said, as his face appeared on the screen, "try searching the Cuddle Buddy Web site. They profile all major Cuddlers—" Kim caught herself. "Er, collectors."

"How'd you know that?" Wade asked.

"I logged on a few times, okay?" Kim said defensively. "They're a good investment."

Wade pulled up the Cuddle Buddy Web site. He clicked to an entry on Amy. "Good call, Kim," said Wade.

Kim scanned the information. "OtterFly is her favorite and . . ." Kim stared at the screen. "She's a biogeneticist?"

"That's not all," Wade went on. "She was kicked out of her university for splicing experiments. Her nickname was DNAmy."

"An out-of-control geneticist," Kim said. She clenched a fist. "I should've paid more attention to Ron's crazed Snow Beast talk. We need to hurry. Wade, is there a satellite that can scan the mountain?"

"Natch," Wade said. "Hoping we might find signs of a hidden scientific lab?"

"If it's not asking too much," Kim replied.

"You're on a roll," Wade told her. "Artificial reinforcements in a large cavern to the north." The screen showed a picture of the site.

"I'm there." Kim put the Kimmunicator in

her pocket and took off on her snowboard. She just hoped that she wasn't too late.

Meanwhile, inside her cavern lab, DNAmy ordered her pig-man and chicken-man to wheel Rufus and Barkin over to a giant machine. It had two small globes—one on each side—and a large center globe with zipperlike notches down the center.

"Wait!" Ron wailed in protest. "Why punish Rufus? Barkin's the one you're mad at!"

"That's it, Stoppable!" Mr. Barkin growled. "You can kiss your two percent good-bye!"

"We could have been so cute together, Stevie," Amy said, as she pulled a pair of green goggles over her eyes. "Well, now you'll find out what it's like to be genetically fused with a hairless rodent."

"Huh?" Barkin looked over at Rufus, who waved. Then he shouted at Amy, "You are one twisted sister!"

The doors on each of the smaller globes opened. A green glow leaked from the machine as Mr. Barkin and Rufus were wheeled inside.

 Mr. Barkin struggled against his straps as the door to his globe hissed closed. Inside the other globe, Rufus's eyes filled with tears, and he waved to Ron. Still strapped to his table, Ron waved back miserably, watching the second door close.

Amy's gloved hands flew across the keyboard. The machinery began to crackle with electricity. A strange green liquid bubbled through a long plastic tube leading to the machine that held Mr. Barkin and Rufus.

Just then, Kim crept into the lab and ducked behind an instrument panel.

Meow.

Kim turned and saw a cat peeking out at her. What a cute kitty, thought Kim. Suddenly, the cat slithered out of the shadows—on a *snake's* body! It reared and hissed.

Uh-oh, thought Kim. Not so cute, after all!

The cat-snake struck, wrapping Kim in its coils. Kim tried to fight, but its grip was too tight. She tripped and fell down the stairs, flying headlong into the wall of plush animals. The snake let go, and Kim grabbed the first two plush toys she saw.

Somersaulting forward, Kim came face-to-face with the crazed scientist. "Let them go, DNAmy!" Kim shouted, holding up the Cuddle Buddies, "or I'll—" Suddenly, Kim noticed what she had in her hand. "Pandaroo!" she cried in a little girl voice.

"SUPERSTAR EDITION? They only made *twelve* of these!"

Oinking and squawking, the pig-man and chicken-man ran toward Kim. She hurled the Cuddle Buddies at them, and the two slid into the wall of plush toys. Half of the huge collection tumbled down on them.

Kim ran toward the scientist, but the Snow Beast jumped to block Kim's path. Amy grinned as the giant rabbit-bear-rhino picked up Kim and hopped over to Amy.

"If you like Cuddle Buddies, Kimmie," Amy said, motioning toward the giant machine that held Mr. Barkin and Rufus, "just wait until you see my genetic zipper in action!"

Machines hummed and sparks flew as Amy threw the switch. Blinding light poured from the genetic zipper. Finally, the machine's doors opened. Out came a huge, muscle-bound mole rat with a bad attitude. It snarled and bared its front teeth.

"Rufus!" Ron cried. "You're a mutant!"

"Gross," Kim said.

"Naked Mole Man," Amy stated proudly as she pulled the ugly creature into a hug, "my greatest splicing success yet!"

Kim looked up at the rabbit-bear-rhino Snow Beast craftily. He still had her in his firm grip. "Hey, Snowy," Kim said, gesturing toward Amy. "Looks like

your Mommy's got a new favorite." The Snow Beast growled. "She doesn't care about you," Kim continued. "You're just another collectible to her."

With a roar, the Snow Beast dropped Kim and bounded toward Naked Mole Man. They rolled over and over, fighting paw-to-paw. Kim didn't waste any time. She ran over to Ron.

"Stop it!" Amy shouted at her mutants. "Stop it this instant! There's room in my heart for all of you!"

The Beast lunged at Naked Mole Man with its horn, but Mole Man dodged out of the way and kicked the Snow Beast backward. The Beast landed against the wall of collectibles, and more plush rained down. Snarling, Naked Mole Man leaped onto a nearby machine and tried to pull it apart. He'd gone berserk!

Quickly, Kim undid the straps that held Ron to the table. "Thanks, K.P.," Ron said. "We've got to get Rufus back."

"And Mr. Barkin!" Kim reminded him.

"Right," Ron agreed. "Him, too."

CHAPTER 9

Pop Rocks

As Naked Mole Man continued to attack the machinery, he ripped off a giant vent and thrust it into another machine.

"No!" Amy cried. "These materials are unstable!"

"Kim!" Wade's voice called from the Kimmunicator. "According to my readings, the whole place is gonna blow!"

Just then, Naked Mole Man picked up Ron.

"Mr. Barkin!" Kim cried. "No!"

But Ron wasn't afraid. "Rufus!" he said to the Naked Mole Man. "I know you're in there, buddy. It's me!" Suddenly, Naked Mole Man's face softened. "That's my Rufus!" Ron said happily. But Naked Mole Man's change of heart didn't last. He began snarling at Ron again.

Kim kicked Naked Mole Man backward, and he fell into the genetic zipper. The doors slid closed. Kim ran to Amy's panel and threw the switch—backward. She had no  idea if it would work, but she had to try.

Energy hummed, and the machine turned red. Finally, the doors slid open. A small naked mole rat peeked out.

"Rufus!" Ron cried as he picked up his

67

pet. "You're okay!" He looked more carefully at his animal friend. He was no longer naked. He was wearing a tiny brown snowsuit. "You're wearing Mr. Barkin's clothes!"

"Then what's Mr. Barkin wearing?" Kim asked.

"Stoppable!" Mr. Barkin shouted from the zipper. "I need pants!"

Kim and Ron couldn't find anything for Mr. Barkin to wear but an old purple bathrobe of Amy's. Mr. Barkin put it on, just as part of the ceiling began to cave in.

"Let's evacuate, people!" Mr. Barkin shouted.

"Just once, I wish the bad guy's lair didn't have to blow up!" Kim griped.

"No!" Amy cried as she ran toward her Cuddle Buddy collection.

Kim grabbed her arm. "You have to leave!"

Amy shook her off. "Not without my Cuddle Buddies!" she shouted, trying to gather them all into her arms.

Just as Kim, Mr. Barkin, Ron, and Rufus ran out of the cave, a deafening explosion let loose, throwing them over the edge of a steep cliff. Luckily, some pine trees broke their fall as Cuddle Buddies rained down from the sky.

"We made it!" Ron cried.

"Great," Kim said. She was glad she'd made it out of the lab alive—but there was something she still had to do. "I need to find my parents and apologize."

The earth began to shake. A low rumbling sound filled the air.

"You might not get the chance," Mr. Barkin said.

"Avalanche!" everyone cried.

They slid down the trees and ran through the snow, pursued by a tidal wave of white.

"We'll never outrun it!" Mr. Barkin said.

Just then, a figure in a puffy red parka appeared on the horizon. He was zooming toward them at an incredible speed. It was Kim's dad on his homemade snowboard!

"No way!" Kim shouted.

"Get ready! No time to stop!" Dr. Possible

shouted, as he scooped the threesome onto his snowboard. "Hang on! This could get 'gnarly'!"

Rocket jets burst into flame at the back of the board, and they ploughed down the mountain just ahead of the avalanche. As they neared a huge gap, Dr. Possible increased the power on the jets and launched across it. The avalanche tumbled after them, falling into the gap, while they landed safely on the other side.

The jet-powered snowboard plunged down a steep slope.

Kim's mother spotted them from the front of the ski lodge. "There they are!" she cried.

"Awesome ride, Dr. P!" Ron shouted as they picked up speed.

Mr. Barkin let out a loud yell as the snow-board shot off the end of a ski slope.

Mr. Barkin covered his eyes and Ron and Rufus shouted, "Whoo-hoo!" as they sailed though the open air. Finally, the group came to a stop, landing upright in front of the lodge. They all stood there a moment, then fell over backward into a heap in the snow.

Kim struggled to sit up. All of the kids in her class were standing in front of the lodge, cheering. They had seen the whole wild ride!

Kim smiled at her father. Then she reached up and wrapped her arms around his neck. He returned her hug, and she knew she had been forgiven.

Funny, thought Kim, for the first time this weekend, I actually wish Bonnie were here to take our picture.

"Dad," said Kim, "you're amazing."

Dr. Possible grinned at his daughter. "Oh, no big," he said.

CHAPTER 10

Mom Rules

A few minutes later, two uniformed police officers escorted DNAmy to a police car. "Come see me, Stevie!" she shouted over her shoulder to Mr. Barkin.

Mr. Barkin cringed.

Amy kissed the glass on the inside of the police car as it pulled away.

Kim looked at her mother, who was still gaping at the strange scene. "Mom, I am so sorry," Kim said.

Kim's mom put her arm around her daughter's shoulders. "Don't worry, honey," she said warmly. "Your father and I were teenagers once. Sometimes we forget what it's like." Then she gave her daughter a warm hug.

Click! A flash went off. "Isn't this a sweet moment. . . ." Bonnie said snidely.

Kim's mom frowned. But it didn't bother Kim in the least.

Just then, a tall, lanky woman with frizzy hair walked out of the lodge. "Bonnie!" she sang.

Bonnie whirled around to face the woman. "Mom?" she cried.

"Pumpkin!" Bonnie's mom chirped happily. She was wearing glasses with purple frames,

purple mittens, purple dangly earrings, and a purple ski sweater. She also had on plaid pants and pink leg warmers.

This was more than a fashion *don't*. It was a fashion *don't even think about it!*

Bonnie's mom pranced over and gave her daughter a tight hug.

Bonnie ducked out of her mom's embrace. "Mother, what are you doing here?" she demanded.

Bonnie's mom pinched her daughter's cheek. "I heard that you kids needed more chaperones, so I rushed right up."

"But . . . you can't!" Bonnie insisted.

"Now, Bon-Bon," Bonnie's mom said, "don't go flying off the handle."

"Bon-Bon?" Ron repeated.

"If everything isn't just so, little Bon-Bon goes straight to pieces," Bonnie's mom said with a laugh.

"But why?" Bonnie squealed, clearly dying of embarrassment. "Who called you?"

"There're too many kids for just us to handle," said Kim's mother. "And I figured if Kimmie got to enjoy having *her* parents around, why not

you, too, Bonnie?" Then Dr. Possible gave Bonnie a sly time-to-take-what-you-dished-out wink.

"This is going to be such fun," Bonnie's mom chirped as she led her daughter away. "You have to introduce me to every single one of your little classmates."

Bonnie closed her eyes and sighed.

Kim couldn't believe it, but she was actually sorry the ski trip was almost over. Oh, well, thought Kim as she watched Bonnie's mother dragging her daughter away, there

would always be Bonnie's yearbook spread to bring back the memories!

Kim smiled up at her own mother. "You rock, Mom," she said.

"You rock, too, Kimmie," said Dr. Possible. Then she wrapped her daughter in the warmest hug ever.